The Ballad of

Audie & Boone

Anne WestWood

ISBN-13: 979-8-218-82349-8

Prologue..4

Chapter One: Jack....................................10

Chapter Two: Where it Began...................19

Chapter Three: Murderers.........................32

Chapter Four: Homesick........................... 44

Chapter Five: Shattered Bottles................ 56

Chapter Six: The Ruby Ring...................... 64

Chapter Seven: Marked in Memphis..........75

Chapter Eight: Beautiful Bruises............... 85

Chapter Nine: Just Peachy........................ 93

Chapter Ten: Cornbread Kisses................ 108

Chapter Eleven: Bullet for Boone............. 114

Chapter Twelve: Salt in Our Wounds........128

Chapter Thirteen: Charleston Shore......... 134

Chapter Fourteen: Empty Cradle.............. 150

Chapter Fifteen: Echoes of Us.................. 159

Epilogue... 162

Prologue

We weren't always like this.

Murderers. Monsters.

Once, we were just two teenagers clawing our way out of
Oatman, Arizona—a town where nobody escapes unless
it's in a body bag or behind the wheel of a stolen car. Or a
horse.

* * *

I was the caregiver. The backbone. The whole damn
support beam. Cooking, cleaning, bathing my sisters,
walking them to school, trying to keep the lights on. My
parents sometimes brought in money, but it always
disappeared chasing their next high.

The night Boone and I started wasn't fate—it was survival for me, and rage for him. We were out of food. My little sisters were crying, clutching their stomachs, voices hoarse from hunger. Ayla and Aria—barely four—were already skin and bones. Their tiny bodies couldn't take another night like that.

I had nine dollars and forty-three cents, scraped from an old makeup bag hidden under my mattress. I prayed it would stretch.

The anger simmered under my skin, not at the twins, but at the world that made me a fourteen-year-old raising children while their dad and my mom nodded off in the next room.

I was a child raising children. And no one was raising me, not even *my* daddy. He'd bailed on us long before then.

Inside the store, it became obvious: I didn't have enough.

Not even for the cheapest box dinners. Not even if I skipped eating and just fed the girls.

So I did what my mom—and every man in my life—taught me to do: *survive dirty*.

I stuffed what I could into my bra and waistband, then walked to the register with only a single can of spaghetti sauce.

Of course, the manager was working that night, and as I made it to the exit, one of the hidden cans had to slip out.

The can crashed to the floor, sauce exploding across the tile.

I froze. Then ran.

But he caught me. Slammed me to the sidewalk with a sickening thud. His grip crushed my arm as if he meant to snap it, his breath hot with the stench of pickles and cheap beef.

"Come here, you little bitch," he hissed, dragging me like I was nothing.

He leaned in close. I saw it in his eyes. He wanted to hurt me.

It reminded me of Dean, Aria, and Ayla's dad.

But what neither of us knew was that Boone Bishop had been sitting on the curb, watching, waiting for an excuse to explode.

He'd come to escape his own hell—his abusive father, dying house, and sad life.

One second, I braced for pain.

Next, the manager hit the pavement.

One punch, out cold.

Boone stood over him, breathing hard.

"You okay?" he asked, sharp with adrenaline.

"Yeah," I said, trying not to shake. "He was an asshole."

"Yeah. For real."

We laughed — like we weren't standing over an unconscious body.

"Audie, right?"

I squinted. "Yeah. Remind me of your name?"

"Boone. Boone Bishop."

And that was it.

After that, it was petty crimes: skipping class, cheating on tests, sneaking cigarettes behind the bleachers.

Boone was a junior. I was in eighth grade.

But we understood each other like no one else ever had.

* * *

A year later, Boone said it was time to stop playing small.

If we wanted out of this sorry town, we had to go bigger.

So we robbed the same market where we met.

And that's how it all began.

Chapter One: Jack

Present

Ding.

The bell gave its usual annoying little shriek as I pranced into the gas station.

It was just a speck on the side of a heat-warped road in the middle of nowhere.

The cashier's eyes started their slow crawl down my body.

Perfect.

Exactly what I wanted.

I chomped my bubblegum loud enough to echo, then leaned on the counter, arms crossed under my chest like I had all the time in the world.

His nametag read Jack.

"Hi, Jack," I said, syrupy sweet. He smiled, right on cue.

"What kinda cigarettes you got?"

He squinted, caught somewhere between suspicion and distraction.

"Are you of age?"

I giggled—light, breathy, a little bored.

"Freshly twenty-one," I lied. "You gonna tell me which ones are best?"

He launched into his sermon—Marlboros, menthols, some off-brand that hits like gravel—I let him talk.

I'd heard it all before. This was our routine.

I played the bait. Boone played with the gun.

Any second now, the bell would scream again, and Boone would step in—revolver raised, voice calm and cold.

And Jack would suddenly forget where he kept the panic button.

And just like that, we'd be gone.

Money in hand, gas tank full, a new state by daylight.

"I'll take the Marlboros," I cut in. I was tired of hearing him talk. Boone was taking longer than usual, and I was ready to get out of there.

"Sure, ID?" Jack said with a flirty little smile.

Ding.

The door let out its whine again as Boone walked in, tall, broad, and carrying his revolver like it was an extension of his damn arm.

His mask was low and worn, leather stretched and cracking from use. His boots thudded heavily against the tile, smelling faintly of dust and gasoline.

That's my man, I thought to myself.

"FREEZE!" he barked.

I dropped to the floor like always—hands on my head, knees to sticky tile.

Part of the show. Part of the dance.

Boone slammed the black duffel on the counter.

"Empty the drawer. Now."

Jack didn't move.

Most of them panic. Beg. Fumble for buttons. But not this one.

He just stared at Boone like he'd already made peace with dying.

"I said now, bitch!" Boone snapped.

That temper of his was always coiled tight, like a lion waiting to pounce.

Somewhere along the way, I'd become his target, his prey—something I never used to be.

He'd snap over nothing, throw things just to hear them break, call me names he swore he didn't mean.

And some nights, when the whiskey hit wrong or the job went south, he'd hit me, too.

But I stayed.

Because love doesn't always show up with flowers and pretty words.

Sometimes it's bruises beneath sleeves and apologies you pretend to believe.

A hand that holds you one minute and punches a hole in the wall the next.

Maybe that's not the kind of love they write songs about, but it was ours, and in my head, that had to count for something.

Jack didn't flinch. Didn't fold.

Instead, he reached under the counter and pulled out his own pistol.

"Sorry, pal," he said, cool and steady. "You picked the wrong gas station today."

My breath caught.

This had never happened before.

Gas stations were supposed to be easy.

I sprang to my feet, fast, charm already loading like a weapon.

Lips pouty. Brown eyes wide. Voice soft and sweet.

"Please," I said, like I meant it. "Just give him the money. He'll hurt us."

But Jack wasn't stupid.

He aimed his gun at me, jaw clenched tight.

He knew.

It could've been the way I looked at Boone.

Or Jack was smarter than the rest.

But Boone noticed, too.

He saw the way Jack's barrel hovered over me.

And he didn't like it.

Not one bit.

The room held its breath as Boone pulled the trigger.

One loud crack.

Jack's body slammed into the cigarette rack, blood blooming across the shelves and wall. His gun slipped from his hand and clattered to the floor.

It all happened fast. Too fast.

I stared at the mess. The air already smelled like copper and smoke.

Poor Jack.

He didn't deserve that.

We weren't supposed to be killers.

"Boone, what the hell?!" I yelled, heart racing. "What are we supposed to do now?"

And for the first time in four years of robbing, running, faking smiles, and dodging bullets… I felt it.

Real, honest fear.

Because this time, I didn't have a damn clue what came next.

Chapter Two: Where it Began

Past

It all started with Boone craving more. He told me it was about the money—cash to get us the hell out, to vanish from this dusty, dead-end town that squeezed the life out of you if you let it.

That could've been true.

However, I believe deeper down, what truly drove him was the need to be in control. His pain was bottled up, and his heart was bruised. He just wanted a fight. Any fight.

And it was better to let him unleash that fury than let it eat him alive.

He wanted us to hit the same grocery store where my life twisted in a new direction—the night I got caught stealing spaghetti sauce. The night the manager tackled me like I was the enemy, and they were a linebacker with a vendetta.

Boone had been sitting on the curb that night, calm and quiet. Watching, waiting for an excuse to swing on someone.

Then, the next thing I knew, he punched that man out cold in one clean hit.

That was the moment everything changed. The moment our words collided.

Now, almost a year later, Boone wanted to go back. Not because it was smart. Not because it was the safest choice. This was personal.

This was about rewriting the story, taking back the power from the scared, hungry girl I used to be. Walking in there no longer as some desperate kid trying not to get caught, but as someone who could take whatever she wanted, and no one would stop her.

"This is the best shot we've got," Boone said, voice low and steady, eyes burning with that wild fire nobody could put out.

"They're the only grocery store in town. They're sitting on a fuckton of cash. If we want out, this is how we do it."

I could've said no. Could've begged him to slow down, to think this through. But hell, I didn't want to.

Boone never took no for an answer anyway. When his mind was made up, trying to stop him was like trying to hold back a freight train with your bare hands. So I said yes. But this time? I wasn't just agreeing. I was all in.

For three days straight, Boone parked himself in the baking asphalt lot, eyes locked on every truck, every employee, every damn customer who walked through those doors.

He memorized shift changes, studied delivery schedules, and noted when the registers were stacked with bills. His jaw was clenched tight, eyes bloodshot from staring too long, nerves wound up so tight you could snap 'em.

Me? I was stuck at the motel, flipping through TV channels without really watching, my heart pulsing with a dangerous kind of excitement. The thrill settled deep in my chest like a live grenade, ticking louder every minute. The stale smell of cigarette smoke clung to the curtains, and the hum of the old AC filled the silence.

At night, Boone barely slept. When he did, his breath was ragged, short, sharp, like gunfire echoing in his dreams. His fists clenched so tight, even in sleep, I swear he was still fighting.

That version of Boone scared the hell out of me.

But damn, did it thrill me, too.

One night, I tried to slow him down.

"Maybe take a breath," I said softly, hoping to cut through the storm inside his head.

He looked at me like I was speaking a foreign language.

"Just fuckin' trust me," he said. And I did.

Because the truth is, I loved it. The danger. The fever that burned through my veins. The way the world sharpened to a knife's edge right before we struck.

I wasn't scared.

I felt electric.

Boone was like a wildfire I couldn't stop reaching for, even when I knew the burn would leave blisters. That tension in his jaw, the way his whole body hummed when a plan clicked, it lit me up. It sent butterflies to my stomach and tingling through my body.

It was the only time I ever really felt *alive*.

The night before the market job, Boone burst through the motel door in a rush, like wind before rain. Shirt half-untucked, knuckles raw and red, eyes wild and darting.

Every thought in his head was racing to the next. I could sense it like I was smelling a fall candle burning.

I grinned because, hell, this was *our* kind of crazy.

"You gonna obsess all night, or you gonna come over here and kiss me?" I teased.

He stopped pacing and looked at me, that fire in his eyes still burning, like I was the only thing that could put it out.

"We're gonna own that store," he said, voice rough and sure.

I didn't ask. I didn't hesitate. I just pulled him close.

We always made love before a job, like sealing a secret pact.

That night, sleep was a joke. Not because of fear, but because of *us*—tangled up, holding tight, every kiss a promise and a dare.

And Boone held me like I was the only thing keeping his ragged edges together.

* * *

At some point, the world went quiet.

Then came the knocks, sharp and quick.

The kind you don't ignore, even in a deep sleep after two intense rounds of love.

Bang.

Bang.

Bang.

I noticed Boone's side of the bed was cold, stiff, and even.

The knocks came again, frantic this time, like someone was losing their mind.

I scrambled to the door, heart pounding, and peeked through the peephole. My hand hovered over the lock for a second, pulse in my ears, before I turned it.

There was Boone, mask on, eyes wild, breath ragged.

I flung the door open.

"Boone! What the hell did you do?"

"Calm down. Don't freak out. I did the job."

"What? You did what?!"

"I watched the store for a week. This was the easiest time to hit it."

"Did anyone see you?"

"That manager—he saw me. He called the cops."

"Shit. I knew this was a bad idea, Boone."

"Damn it, Audie, don't judge me, we gotta go."

We grabbed our five bags and bolted to the parking lot.

The Arizona heat hit us like a furnace, waves rolling off the cracked blacktop.

"We need to steal a car. Something fast. Preferably."

"Are you serious?"

"Yeah. You wanted to rob a grocery store. That comes with side hustles."

I rolled my eyes so hard I thought my skull would crack.

Boone's eyes locked on a '06 Dodge Charger—black, matte finish, muscle curves ready to pounce.

"That one," he said, voice gravelly.

Boone pulled a small toolkit from his pocket and got to work.

No keys, no problem.

His fingers twisted wires, stripping and rewiring with an ease that looked like art.

Minutes later, the engine came alive.

It was a beast ready to tear through the desert.

It rumbled beneath us as we peeled out of the lot, dust and danger chasing us down.

The road ahead was wide open.

And whatever came next, well, we'd face it together.

"Where are we headed, Boone?"

"We're gonna have to leave. For good this time. Maybe head south."

My heart sank.

I knew my life in Oatman wasn't good—not even close—but it was all I'd ever known for fifteen years.

Leaving meant turning my back on everything: my family, my blood.

Most of all, leaving meant turning my back on Ayla and Aria.

But something shifted in me right then. A switch was flipped.

I went numb to the past, to the house I grew up in, to the pieces of a life I'd tried so hard to keep together.

I loved my sisters. I even loved my mama, in that complicated way you love someone who never loved you right.

But I knew if I didn't get out now, I never would.

And Boone?

Boone was my shot.

He kept me fed, alive, loved, and clothed—more than my parents ever could.

I'd heard the saying my whole life: "People only escape Oatman three ways: crime, death, or fame."

I never imagined that old town tale would apply to me.

But it did.

It applied to both of us.

Crime got us out.

And it never let us look back at that soul sucking town

again.

Chapter Three: Murderers

Present

The lines on the highway kept flashing by like nothing had happened.

The desert didn't care about Jack. It just kept rolling on, dried out and empty. Like a God attempted to build something once and gave up halfway through.

Maybe that's what Boone and I were now, half-finished things abandoned by whatever God that was supposed to love us.

My hands shook in my lap, fingers crusted with cheap gas station blood that stank of pennies and panic.

Boone's knuckles clenched the wheel so tight I thought the leather might tear.

Neither of us spoke for a long time.

Outside, the desert blurred—dry and sunbitten, not a damn thing alive.

Inside, the air turned hot and thick, mean even.

The car reeked of sweat and gasoline, but there was something else, too.

Something wicked.

Like whatever happened back there had followed us into the car and curled up in the backseat.

"I keep seeing his face," I whispered.

Boone didn't look at me. He just muttered, "He pulled first."

But I kept seeing it anyway.

Jack's face.

Not scared.

Just… surprised.

Like he didn't think it'd actually happen.

Like he thought we were just two kids messing around.

He was on the ground in no time, and there was blood.

So much blood. The red splatter on the tile, too familiar, like that night with the spaghetti sauce. It got everywhere: my hands, my jeans, my shoes… and later, it stayed under my nails for weeks, no matter how hard I scrubbed.

Like he'd worked his way into me.

The weight of what we'd done was catching up to me.

"But we weren't supposed to kill anybody," I said, my voice cracking around it. "That wasn't the plan."

"There is *no* plan, Audie," he snapped, voice stern. "The plan is to survive. That's it."

His thumb tapped the wheel once. Twice.

It was his nervous tic.

"We head south," he added, eyes never leaving the road.

South. Of course.

That bank in Atlanta. The one he's been dreaming about for months—hell, maybe a year.

He talked about it like it was some promised land, like if we could just hit that one jackpot, everything would reset.

We'd be new people.

Clean people.

Only I didn't believe in clean anymore.

Not after what we did to Jack.

"You think the news has it yet?" I asked.

Quieter now.

"You think they're saying our names?"

Boone's jaw twitched.

"Doesn't matter. We're ghosts now."

No, I thought. *We're murderers now.*

But I didn't say it.

I was too scared to see the look on his face if I did.

I pressed my forehead to the window. The glass was scorching hot.

The desert just kept stretching—empty, dry, dead.

Just like Jack.

I couldn't tell if I was crying or just sweating.

"What'd you do with… the body?" I felt the lump rising in my throat as I said it.

Boone kept driving.

Didn't answer right away.

Then:

"I dragged him to the back. Wiped the counter. Busted the cameras. Same shit as always. Only messier."

Only deadlier, I thought.

No more pretending this is just some thrill ride. We were outlaws now.

"So if we're heading south, where exactly are we going?" I asked.

Like I didn't already know, like I hadn't known for months now.

Boone'd been talking about Atlanta like it was holy. It was like the end of the tunnel.

The bank.

The plan.

He never said the word *plan* out loud, but I knew.

I could see it in the way he moved when he talked about it. He'd get that twitch in his jaw, the hungry look in his eyes.

But Boone hated it when I disagreed, and I would still tell him that it wasn't smart. When I did, he would blow up—yelling, cussing, hollering like a damn storm.

And eventually, what started as thunder turned to bruises.

Just a few days before, we were holed up in some trash motel off I-10, arguing about money. He hadn't eaten all day—said it made him mean.

I told him that there was no excuse to treat me the way he had been.

He backhanded me so fast, I didn't even know what happened 'til I tasted blood.

He cried and sobbed. Said he hated himself for it. Swore he'd never do it again, like he always did.

But his promises always sounded sweet and tasted sour.

I didn't blame him… not really.

His single daddy had raised him mean, quick with his hands. But Boone, the seventeen-year-old boy I met with busted smiles and broken bones, had grown into something sharper.

And me?

I was now an eighteen-year-old girl with no family and no way out.

Raised by silence, chased by my past.

Trying to keep both of us alive.

I still believed—somehow, stupidly—that Boone could heal.

If I just held on long enough.

If I just stayed quiet enough.

If I just stopped making him so mad.

Then he would heal.

Maybe I was just as bad, just as broken.

I stayed, didn't I?

Kept loving him like rocking a snake to sleep and calling it mine.

Maybe that made me loyal, or maybe just too stubborn to run.

But I don't think it was a weakness.

He needed me, and I chose to stay.

Nobody else ever did that for him.

And ain't nobody ever done that for me, either.

* * *

"How 'bout we hit the bank in Atlanta," he said, like he was offering me a gift, "and then go to Charleston?"

I turned toward him, heart fluttering.

Charleston.

"I think I can get us a place," he added. "Right on the beach. What do you think?"

Boone was always thoughtful in the wrong ways.

He remembered that dream I had—the beach house, the soft air, the quiet.

The way I used to talk about seashells and porches and salt on our skin.

But dreams rot when you drag blood through them.

Still. How could I say *no* to that?

Even if the ocean couldn't wash us clean.

"Aw, Boone," I whispered. "That's perfect,"

But it hit me, *how the hell will we afford that?*

Will the heist really give us that much money?

"You really think the heist'll cover all that? And keep us under the radar for a while?"

He grinned. Wild and crooked.

"Yes, baby. You don't understand. This is the biggest bank in the South. This *is* the jackpot."

He was right.

And it turned me on in all the wrong ways.

It made me feel alive again, even if just for a second.

Even if I knew it was all gonna crash and burn.

We were headed toward something big—Atlanta—and I could feel it pulling us in.

But Jack's blood would still be there.

No matter how far we ran, it would cling to us—on our hands, in our clothes, and deep in our souls.

Chapter Four: Homesick

Past

When I was little, I used to dream about running away with someone who loved me.

Not a prince. Not a knight. Just someone who gave a damn.

Someone who'd hold my face like it was soft, not broken.

Someone who didn't leave, like my daddy did to my momma and me.

We didn't know it then, but that night was the calm before everything split wide open.

One crusty motel room. Two cups of ramen that we stole earlier that day.

Boone's T-shirt was swallowing me whole.

The air conditioner was wheezing like it was dying—but hell, it was cold, and we were clean, and for once, I wasn't scared.

For a minute, we weren't thieves.

We weren't poor.

We weren't broken kids who grew up too fast in a town that didn't care if we lived or died.

For a minute, we were just us.

Boone Bishop and Audie Carter.

Laughing. Free. Full.

"You like playing house?" he asked, voice low, hands creeping around my waist.

I smiled. "You like pretending you're the man of one?"

He didn't answer. Just pulled me back against his chest, lips on my neck, breath in my ear.

"You don't get it," he said. "You're mine, Audie. Always have been."

I should've rolled my eyes.

Instead, I melted.

Because Boone didn't say sweet things the way normal people did.

His version of *I love you* was saying *you're mine*, and I accepted that.

He kissed me hard—no warning, no easing in—just a hand sliding under the shirt and pulling it over my head, like any space left between us was a betrayal he wouldn't tolerate.

"I need every damn part of you," he whispered, jerking me closer with his scarred arms. His veins flowed down them like rivers carved deep into his skin.

There wasn't a piece of me left untouched that night.

Soft wasn't in Boone.

Maybe that's why I loved him so damn much.

Because beneath all that hard, angry edge was something fierce and real.

Something I couldn't walk away from, even if I wanted to.

He always kissed like he wanted to hurt me just a little, probably to see if I wanted to stay.

And I did.

Because when he touched me like that—rough, certain, desperate…I felt wanted.

The motel was cheap, the walls were thin, and the bed was loud.

But we didn't give a damn.

It was just us, tangled in our sweaty skin, wrapped up in our own broken world.

Afterward, Boone stayed pressed against me, his fingers trailing lines down my spine like he was still claiming me.

"You don't need anybody else," he whispered.

"I'll always keep you safe, Audie, I promise." It was almost like he was giving me his own fucked up vows right then and there.

I turned into his chest, heart still pounding like a warning I couldn't read.

"I know that," I said.

And I meant it.

Even if it would end up killing me.

"We'll never go back to Oatman, not ever."

"I know that, too."

"And we'll never talk to anyone from Oatman ever again."

I didn't know that part. I wanted to talk to my sisters, and in my mind, that could still happen somehow.

"You do know that, right, Audie?"

"Yeah, I know. Fuck Oatman!"

I played along, but really, I was *crushed*.

* * *

Boone had passed out shortly after we were done talking. He was worn out from the sex, being awake for two days

straight, and from all the whiskey he'd been drinkin'
recently.

I knew it would be my one and only chance to talk to my
sisters for the last time.

I sat there a moment, staring at the landline like it might
bite. If Boone woke up, I was done for.

Boone was amazing, truly, but he was being so
controlling with the "rules" about home. I understood
why, to an extent, but I was all my poor baby sisters had.

I finally picked up the motel phone and dialed my
momma's home number: *(555) 019-4827.*

I couldn't forget it. All the times I had to dial it because
nobody picked me up from school, a friend's house,
practice, tutoring, *literally everything.*

The tone buzzed once. Twice.

Click.

"Yeah?" Her voice came through sharp and slurred. It was familiar in the worst way.

I froze. My hand tightened around the landline. Her voice hit like a punch to the gut.

"…Momma?"

A beat of silence.

Then a dry laugh. "Well, look who finally decided to call."

My throat closed. I didn't know what I expected, maybe worry. Something motherly.

But I should've known better.

"I just—" I swallowed. "I just wanted to check on Ayla and Aria."

"They're fine." Her voice clipped, irritated. "Sleeping. Unlike me."

I could already picture her: half-drunk, half-awake, fresh track marks lining her arms, bitterness rolling off her tongue.

"You sure?" I asked, voice cracking despite me. "You've been taking care of them? Taking them to school? Giving 'em baths?"

Another silence.

Then: "Don't you dare call here acting high and mighty, Audie Rose. You ran off with that no-good boy like a goddamn fool, and now you wanna play mom?"

"I'm just asking if they're okay."

"They're fine. Better now that you're not around to drag them into your mess."

I didn't say anything. Just listened to her harsh, uneven breathing.

Then: "Boone's got you out there on the run, doesn't he?" Her voice turned cruel. "Told you he was trash. Same as his no-good daddy, Bruce."

I flinched. Looked at Boone, asleep and still breathing steadily beside me.

"I gotta go," I whispered.

"Don't call here again unless you grow the hell up."

Click.

The line went dead.

I stared at the landline for a second longer than I needed to. Then gently, like it might break, I hung it up.

Boone stirred, eyes still heavy with sleep, but he reached for me without looking.

I crawled into his arms like muscle memory.

He held me tight against his chest, one hand running down my back slowly and steadily, almost like he knew.

Maybe he did.

I buried my face in his shirt, heart cracking quietly.

I couldn't stop my mind from racing: *Boone was right—fuck Oatman, fuck everyone in that town. We didn't need them.*

I'd never call back there again. Not ever.

It tore at me, knowing I'd never hear their voices again. But when you're running from your past, some things can't come with you.

The motel was cold, Boone's arms were warm, and somewhere miles away, my sisters were asleep without me.

That was the night I learned you can feel homesick for

people you'll never see again.

And for the first time in a long time, I cried myself to

sleep that night.

Chapter Five: Shattered Bottles

Present

The car rolled to a stop in front of the liquor store, its flickering neon sign humming like a bad omen.

Boone's fingers tapped the steering wheel—hungry, restless.

I swallowed the knot that rose in my throat.

If it ain't obvious by now, robbing places was just how we got by. Usually, it was for money, but that night Boone had a side mission: liquor.

We'd put about 500 miles behind us and crossed into a new state—New Mexico. Some locals called it the Land of Enchantment, like that meant something.

Personally, I thought it looked like the Land of Nothing.

Out there, it was just heat and dirt and silence, same as Arizona.

I wondered how far the desert went. It felt like it stretched on forever, like one of those old songs that keeps playing when you open a dusty jewelry box. Haunting. Endless.

Boone started loading his revolver. His jaw flexed with every click, like he was biting back something ugly. I knew what came next.

He'd load mine, I'd stuff it into my panties, and strut in first—play the part, distract the employees, stall until Boone came in to finish the job.

Sure enough, that's exactly how it went. Almost like I was a psychic.

The door screeched its same ole song behind me as I stepped into the store and locked eyes with a handsome Hispanic man stocking shelves near the register.

I started my slow strut down each aisle, giving Boone time to prep.

His eyes followed me like I was either a curse or an angel. I didn't mind being both.

As I turned the corner into the next aisle, I nearly ran into another employee.

Great, I thought. Guess I'm gonna have to get my hands dirty this time.

"Oops—sorry! I'm such a ditz," I said, turning on my perfect little charm.

He grinned widely, ear to ear.

"No worries, ma'am. Need help finding anything?"

"No, no, just looking around. Thank you, though," I said, tossing him a wink as I wiggled on through.

I could feel my denim shorts riding up my thighs, but I didn't fix them.

I knew it was working in my favor.

I spotted two other customers: a younger guy in the next aisle eyeing the beer cooler, and an older woman heading toward the register with a bottle of red wine.

Neither of them knew their lives were about to change forever.

Then it came—that screech again—and Boone Bishop burst through the door, pistol raised, face hidden behind his worn black ski mask.

I could see his eyes through the holes. Soulless. Empty. Scary.

I kind of hoped he'd recognize me in the chaos.

"EVERYONE DOWN!"

We dropped—like we'd rehearsed it. My pulse hammered in my ears, so loud it almost drowned out Boone's voice.

The customers dropped beside me.

The employee closest to the door raised his hands but stayed standing. Bad idea.

Boone was unpredictable, especially these days.

"DROP TO YOUR KNEES!" Boone barked again, pistol aimed straight at the man's head.

"Don't hurt anybody, please," the employee said. Not defiant, just stupid.

That's when I saw the other employee, army crawling toward the register. Probably trying to hit the panic button.

Boone didn't notice him, but he was getting closer by the second.

I couldn't let that happen.

So I did what any loyal woman would do—I pulled my revolver from my panties and shot him in the back.

I didn't mean to kill him.

But I did mean to stop him.

And I wasn't ashamed of that.

That's when shit went sideways.

The second I fired, the old lady let out a scream—high, raw, and panicked, like a desperate prayer ripped from her throat.

The employee near Boone didn't even get the chance to move. One shot to the head, and he was done.

The young man came at me fast, fists flying like I'd killed his brother.

I didn't want to kill that kid. Hell, he was just a boy buying beer—wrong place, wrong time.

But when he started pounding on me—punching, kicking, full of rage—I didn't have a choice.

I'm not strong enough to go blow for blow with a man that size.

So I shot him, too.

And the old lady? Just a poor, innocent witness. A ghost who saw too much.

We couldn't let her live. Not with what she'd seen.

Boone handled it—cold, quiet, deadly.

It was a fucking bloodbath.

We found one of the dead man's Astravans parked out front—the perfect ride to haul everything and disappear.

I grabbed the cash from the register while Boone smashed the cameras and loaded up a shit-ton of liquor.

Then we packed the bodies into the back of the van.

We drove out into the desert, far enough to burn every last trace in a bonfire big enough to light up the whole damn sky.

When the flames died down, we buried the bones deep in the dust.

And just like that, they were gone.

Like whispers in the wind.

Like they'd never been there at all.

Boone drove calmly through the haunted desert, like the night hadn't swallowed four lives.

Chapter Six: The Ruby Ring

Past

I should've said no.

Should've pointed out that we had enough trouble just living, we didn't need the law on our backs, too.

But he had that look on his face, the same one he always wore.

That one that said: Stop me, I dare you.

And I knew there was no stopping Boone. He was reckless, but that was one of my favorite things about him.

Hell, that's probably why I fell in love with him.

We'd broken into places before. Stores, sheds, people's homes.

Not proud of it, but even a church once.

However, this felt different.

More dangerous.

Because it was more dangerous.

Some half-assed plan Boone cooked up in the back of an abandoned bowling alley, his eyes lit up, fingers twitching with that little tic of his.

"Pawn shop on Lincoln," he said, voice low like a dare, a grin tugging at his mouth.

"Owner's old as dirt. Closes early. We'll be in and out before the dust even notices."

So we went.

Middle of the night. Dark hoodies. Cheap gloves. One crowbar between us.

Wasn't even supposed to be a full job—just a small enough hit to get us by a few more days.

But the back door was unlocked, buying us more time than we should've had.

And Boone had a side mission, of course, he always did. I just didn't know about this one at the time.

He was on the hunt for a ruby ring… for me.

And when Boone found that door unlocked, well, he just couldn't help himself.

"I'll be quick," he said.

That should've been the moment I turned around.

Ran.

Waited by the road.

But I didn't.

I followed him in, and we were like two kids in a candy shop.

The air was thick with dust and mildew, like even the town had turned its back on the place.

He cracked the register first, pried it open with the crowbar like he'd done it a hundred times before. Bills fluttered out like it was easy, like crime was just second nature.

"Check the case," he said, nodding toward a row of glass boxes lined with dusty jewelry and cracked electronics.

"Bet half this shit ain't even real." He said, laughing under his breath.

I crouched low, my pulse a drum in my ears. Boone was right—half the gold was flaking already.

Probably fake as hell.

But I didn't care.

We needed cash, not diamonds.

A creak somewhere behind us made my breath hitch, but it was only the old building settling. I hated how my hands shook when I reached for the next piece.

I'd just stuffed as much as I could into my hoodie pocket when the sirens began outside.

"Boone," I hissed.

He looked up, and I didn't even have to say it.

He heard it, too, now.

That distant wail, soft at first, but growing louder by the second.

The kind of sound that twists your gut before it even reaches the street.

Boone's face barely flickered. Then, quick and sharp, he sprang into action. Busting the cameras, shoving bills into the duffle bag, and slamming the register closed like we hadn't just emptied it.

"Back door," he roared.

But just as we walked out, blue and red lights peeked through the buildings.

Cops.

"Shit," I whispered.

Boone grabbed my arm. Hard.

"Run."

His voice was low, urgent.

"What?"

"I said run, Audie. Now."

I froze—just for a second.

He shoved the duffel in my hands, kissed me hard, and that was all it took.

I bolted like hell.

Somewhere behind me, I heard the cops yelling, "Hands where I can see 'em!"

I ran faster. I had to.

I couldn't get caught.

But I knew either way, Boone wasn't gonna let that happen.

Next thing I knew, he was calling my burner phone from the Maricopa County Jail, asking me to bail him out with the exact money we'd just risked everything to steal.

"Hey, baby, you okay? Where are you?"

"Hi, baby. I'm fine. Been holed up at that same motel—y'know, before the shop. You good there?"

"Yeah, yeah, I'm fine. Don't worry 'bout me, babe. But I do need you to bail me out."

I sighed. "Boone. How am I supposed to do that?"

"With the money."

He was trying to hint.

"But that's our money for food, Boone. We can't just blow it all on bail."

"So you're just gonna leave me in here?" His voice turned sharp and accusatory. I knew what he meant. We were gonna have to do something else illegal soon.

But all I could think was—what if we got caught again?

"No, of course not. I'll figure it out, babe."

Like I always do, I thought to myself.

"Thank you, sugar," he said, soft all of a sudden. "I'd burn the whole damn world down for you, baby."

Then the call was cut off. Sharp. Like a knife to the gut.

That's just how it goes in jail.

I took a minute. I gathered my thoughts, then the cash. Then I headed to the station and slapped five grand—the only five grand we had—on the counter like some twisted love letter.

He had a quick sit-down with some fancy woman who handed him a court date he'd never bother showing up for.

That was his first warrant, by the way. I was still naive, trying to clean up his messes, though there was no cleaning up that one.

But when he saw me, that boy lit up like I hung the damn moon.

Boone came busting through that steel door like nothing had changed.

Same old grin. Same old swagger.

His cracked lips stretched into that crooked grin, teeth all spaced out and wild.

He ran right at me, picked me up, spun me around like some movie ending, then kissed me like we were the only two people left on earth.

"I love you," he said.

I just blinked at him. I'd waited two years to hear those words from his deep, gravel-sickened voice.

And now? I was stunned and silent.

"I love you too, Boone," I finally said, voice soft like it might break.

I felt my cheeks get hot. Blushing. Me. I never blushed.

But this time I did. Because this time, it felt real. It felt like ours.

We climbed into our beat-up Ford F-150 and got the hell out of Maricopa.

The tires chewed up the road, and Boone grinned like the world was his to burn.

Chapter Seven: Marked in Memphis

Present

It was the first time in forever that we didn't leave a body behind.

But it was also the first time the world let us know it was watching.

Boone and I had agreed to hit the grocery store before we crossed the Memphis–Arkansas Bridge, just shy of midnight.

It was one of those nothing towns, you know the kind. A few busted streetlights, a Dollar General, and folks who leave their doors unlocked because they still believe the world's mostly good.

But it ain't.

Not when people like us are passing through.

Boone and I needed cash. And *food*.

And nothing—not Jesus, not luck, not some half-asleep cashier—was gonna stop us.

I was behind the wheel tonight, the getaway driver. I'd done this before.

I usually just did whatever Boone told me to do, and I didn't mind.

The air was thick and muggy, and the shadows in the streets stretched long like they already knew what was coming.

Boone jumped out of the car and walked in, relaxed, mask on, revolver in hand.

My head jerked from side to side, making sure the coast was clear.

The getaway driver meant you were also on the lookout.

I watched through the tinted windows as Boone threatened the sleepy cashier with his shiny, freshly cleaned pistol. The trembling worker emptied every register and a small safe... we hit a big one.

Sprinting back to the van, Boone grabbed a bunch of sandwiches and candy bars—food for the next couple of days.

As we sped off, Boone yelled abruptly, "STOP! We need to switch cars!"

"What?! Right now?"

"Yes, we need a new ride."

He pointed to an old Nissan Altima. It wasn't much, but it did the job, and we were off.

But we weren't smart enough to check the tank, and we were running low, fast.

"We're gonna have to stop, Boone. If not, we're gonna be stuck on the side of the road."

"Okay, okay. Stop at the station off this exit."

And I did—because I obeyed him.

As we pumped gas and stretched our legs, that's when the world wanted to remind us it was watching.

"Hey! You're those two outlaws they've been posting everywhere!" A stranger yelled from across the lot—tall, wiry, with a voice rough as gravel and a trucker cap pulled so low I couldn't see his eyes.

I looked at Boone. I thought, *this can't be real*. And for half a second—just a flicker—I wondered what would happen if I jumped into the car, sped off, and left Boone standing there. Then I shoved it down, because the reality was we were both in too deep.

"Audie and, um, what was it... Boone! Yeah, from Arizona!"

Boone grabbed my arm so hard he practically threw me into the car, and we were gone within three seconds.

I could hear the man in the distance telling his wife to call the cops. A car door slammed somewhere close. A dog barked. Every sound felt like it was rushing toward us.

"WE'RE ON THE NEWS? OUR NAMES?" I screeched, tires screaming with me as Boone sped off.

"Breathe, Audie. It's okay. It'll die down quickly. That was just one person."

"I bet they know we killed those people. We're going to prison."

"Audie, I will never let that happen. I'd kill myself before I went to prison, do you understand me?"

His words stung worse than a bee, but I understood.

"Me too."

And that night, we made an unspoken pact: We'd die before we let them see us desperate. We'd never die begging.

The road stretched ahead, black as sin, endless as the sea. Behind us, the city lights faded, and the weight of what just happened struck like a judge's gavel on my heart.

We weren't just running from our past anymore—we were running from the law... and ourselves.

And there was no turning back.

* * *

By morning, my eyes were bloodshot from the marijuana and from crying after all our arguing.

We'd driven through the night, arguing nonstop because Boone wanted to keep living this crooked life.

I understood where he was coming from—this was all we'd ever known.

But I tried to tell him, "Baby, we're only eighteen and twenty-one. It's not too late to change our lives."

He refused to listen.

His whole damn face was still lit up red, just like a tomato. And he hadn't let off the gas once, doing a hundred through the night like he was trying to outrun the fight we just had.

I didn't say a word.

Let him stew.

I thought: *At least we were getting to Georgia quicker.*

At least the job was waiting.

At least there'd be something to focus on that wasn't us falling apart in real time.

We were in the great state of Mississippi. Nearly twenty-five hours and about 1,700 miles from home.

Boone and I had never been this far before—never left the desert long enough to see what green actually looked like.

Back in Oatman, everything was cracked and brittle: sunburnt hills, rusted-out trailers, wind that howled like it hated you.

But here? Mississippi was a whole different kind of wild.

The air was wet enough to drink, thick with heat, and reeked of mud and magnolia.

Trees hung low and heavy, like they were gathering intel for the police.

Vines crawled over every fence post, broken-down building, and street light, like nature was trying to bury the past and start over.

The roads wound through backwoods, long and lonely, with nothing but gas stations, closed-down churches, and bugs big enough to look back at you.

It felt like we were driving through the belly of something alive.

And still—300 miles to go before we hit Georgia.

Our biggest job yet.

And our faces were out there now. On gas station TVs, convenience store doors, maybe even in someone's prayers.

I don't know if it was the weed, the liquor, the bruised-up kind of love we called ours, or that twitch in your gut you get when you know the clock's damn near outta sand…

But somehow, we still convinced ourselves it was a good idea.

That this was the *only* way to have the life we've always wanted.

Deep down, I think we knew better.

At least I did.

I just didn't want to say it out loud.

Chapter Eight: Beautiful Bruises

Past

I swear I still had a tiny piece of that scared little girl inside me—until that night.

That godforsaken abandoned house Boone and I crashed in for nine long months, just two broken kids scraping by on cold coffee and long nights.

Some nights it creaked like it had its heartbeat. That night, I heard a knock—soft, slow—like someone testing the walls from the inside. Boone didn't notice. Or maybe he pretended not to.

It wasn't the busted heater or the pipes coughing up brown water, or even the way we'd been rationin' our damn canned beans like it was treasure.

No, it was the second I asked Boone if we had any cash left that he finally snapped—like all that slow-burning rage bottled up inside him just blew wide open.

And there I was, standing in the mess of it, knowing this was the moment everything between us started to bleed.

"Why do you always gotta do that shit like you don't trust me?" Boone accused, standing up and grinding his cigarette out on the old, original wooden floorboards.

"Baby, I do trust you. I never said I didn't. I just—" My hoarse voice trailed off.

I'd been scared of Boone before, hell, hundreds of times.

But I'd never feared for my safety because of Boone… until this moment.

"You just what, Audie?"

"I just wanted to know. To see if maybe we could get out of here. A motel. Some more food. Something better than this."

That's when I hit a nerve. The one he'd been barely holding onto inside himself. Boone's jaw ticked. He started pacing, slow at first, his boots scuffing the floor, cigarette burning down between his fingers.

And then he let it all loose on me.

"OH, SO I DON'T PROVIDE FOR YOU? Is that what you're saying?"

I shook my head, too shocked to speak.

He grabbed the empty Jack Daniel's bottle lying beside the blankets we used as a mattress and flung it across the room. It shattered against the wall, glass shattering like his broken promises.

"You don't have to do that, you know!" I
shouted—scared, but finally done letting his rage own the
room. I was hoping that standing my ground might work.
It used to, sometimes, when Ayla and Aria's dad got like
that.

"DO WHAT, EXACTLY?" he spat back, voice thick,
nearly spitting the words at me.

"Try to scare me."

I should've never said that.

As soon as those words floated across the room, he came
crashing down on me.

And not in the usual way.

Not the kind that ended with him laughing in my neck.

He was swinging. Cussing. Flinging every insult he had
in him.

He was like a bomb ready to go off at any second.

His hands gripped tightly around my throat. I was gasping, seeing stars, when his ocean-blue eyes locked on mine—the same eyes that he used to call pretty.

I wondered if they still looked pretty with the fear all over 'em.

Then his grip eased, and he eventually let go of my neck.

Everything went still.

I don't know why.

Maybe it was the look on my face.

Maybe he just got bored.

Or maybe he was just too damn tired to finish the job.

I didn't even fight back. I just let it happen.

And I would've been dead—hell, I was real close.

By the time it was over, my left eye was swollen shut, blood in my mouth, and bruises spreading across every inch of me.

He blinked.

His whole face was shattered with regret.

"Fuck. Audie—fuck—I didn't mean—"

He backed away like he'd set himself on fire.

"I swear to God, baby, I didn't mean to—fuck—" His hands trembled.

"I'm sorry. I'm so fucking sorry."

He dropped like he'd been shot, crumpling to the floor with his head in his hands, sobbing so hard it almost felt like I was the one who'd done something wrong.

"I'm a monster," he whispered. "You should go. I wouldn't blame you."

But I didn't move.

I stood there, breathing through the sting, watching the only person I ever loved fall apart.

And I thought: *It ain't him. It's the world. His abusive daddy, that no-good runaway mama—we were both broken before we even found each other.*

I knelt beside him and placed my hand on his back.

"I'm not going anywhere," I said. "I'm staying right here."

He wouldn't look at me—probably 'cause of how bad my face looked—but he grabbed my hand and started rubbing it, whispering, "Audie Rose, I'd rather die than lose you, and I swear I'll never hit you again. I'm so sorry."

Tears spilled from his eyes again.

A lump stuck in my throat, and a tear slipped down my cheek.

I wiped it away quickly before he could see.

I loved Boone.

I cared for him deeper than I cared for myself.

Being with Boone Bishop was a damn roller coaster—high, low, and hell in between.

And one thing was for sure: that night wasn't the last time he laid hands on me.

Not even close.

Chapter Nine: Just Peachy

Present

We hit Georgia around dusk, the highway humming under us like it knew where we were headed.

Atlanta was still just a dot on the map, but it was getting bigger by the minute. An hour out, maybe less.

One big city.

One big job.

Then freedom, if you believe in that sort of thing.

Boone sure did. He'd been talking nonstop since Birmingham.

About the beach house, about a fresh start and ocean air, about sleepin' in and makin' pancakes like we were already safe.

I let him talk.

But my mind was on the stakeout. On how fast the cops in a place like Atlanta could swarm a scene.

We pulled into a busted-up gas station just past Douglasville, and that's when I saw it.

A palm tree.

Fake as hell, probably plastic.

Just one, leaning up against a taco shack that looked about two weeks from being condemned.

But still, it stopped me cold.

Boone laughed, all teeth.

"Ain't that a sign, baby?"

Maybe it was.

But it felt more like a joke.

Like Georgia was dressing up, pretending to be something better, just like we were.

I gave an awkward laugh, "... yeah."

We loaded back up in the old Nissan and took the back roads, which were half-lit with nothing. It was Boone's idea, of course.

He loved the good ole country roads, probably because he felt like we were two ghosts disappearing from the chaos we'd created.

Every minute that went by, we got closer to Atlanta. And before we knew it, Boone was booking us a room at some raggedy motel west of the city.

He paid cash and flirted with the lady at the front desk like we weren't two wanted kids on the edge of doin' something incredibly stupid.

I stood off to the side, hood up, eyes down, countin' cars in the lot—four, and that was including ours.

The room smelled like bleach, trying to cover up mildew, crime, and affairs.

One crooked lamp in each corner, a stained comforter, and a TV bolted to the dresser that only played static and preachers… *maybe we needed one of those*, I thought to myself.

Boone flopped down on the bed like it was a damn resort. "Home sweet home."

I didn't sit. Just walked to the window, peeled back the curtain, and took inventory—three cars, one busted streetlight, and a vending machine wheezing like it might give up at any second.

"We'll watch the bank tomorrow," I said. "Morning shift, lunch crowd, afternoon deliveries."

Boone yawned like we were talking bedtime stories.

"Damn, Sugar. Are you already planning? We just walked in."

I looked back at him. "We're not here to relax."

He barked a laugh, loud and sharp. "Do you ever stop thinking long enough to breathe?"

I didn't say a word.

Didn't have to.

Because no... I didn't.

Not anymore.

Boone turned onto his side, arm draped across his stomach, eyes closed like he could fall asleep right then and there.

Like we weren't days away from goin' full *Bonnie and Clyde*.

"You know what I want first?" he mumbled. "Once it's all done."

I didn't ask, but he told me anyway.

"I want a big-ass steak. Not that gray shit you gotta drown in ketchup. And mashed potatoes… real ones, made by you. The kind that comes out so creamy, they don't need anything else. DAMN, I want a kitchen again. A real one. Cold beer, running water, and a working stove that we can actually use."

He talked about kitchens like other men talked about motorcycles and paradise—probably 'cause he never had one that wasn't full of mold or mice.

He smiled like he was already there.

I stayed quiet. The air conditioner growled through the wall, louder than it was cold. I could hear voices through the paper-thin wall next door—someone cussing, something slamming.

Boone didn't flinch.

"Don't that sound nice?" he said.

I finally sat down on the edge of the bed, facing him. I flashed him a half smile.

"Yeah. Real nice."

It wasn't a lie, exactly. I just didn't let myself picture it.

Didn't feel safe wishin' for things.

Didn't feel safe at all.

When you go wishin' for things, that's when your heart gets broke.

I've been down that road too many times, and I refuse to go down it again.

The room grew quiet except for the air conditioner's rattling and the muffled arguments next door.

Boone's chest rose and fell steadily, like he'd already slipped into sleep—the one you fake so the nightmares don't catch you.

I stayed sitting on the edge of the bed, eyes fixed on the cracked ceiling. The peeling paint looked like the scars we both carried—patchy, raw, barely hanging on.

I thought about that steak, about those mashed potatoes, about all the simple things Boone wanted but never had. A kitchen. Cold beer. Runnin' water.

Hell, I wanted those things too.

But I was too scared to say it out loud. Because that meant I had a dream, and poor people like me don't get to dream.

Instead, I pulled my hoodie tighter around me and stared out the window at the parking lot—the three cars, the broken streetlight, the humming vending machine—like they were all the world I could trust right now.

* * *

We woke before dawn, the kind of dark that feels like it's watching you back. Boone moved quickly and quietly—no nonsense. I grabbed the binoculars, checked my gear, and tried to steady my breath, which kept catching in my throat.

The Nissan eased into a cracked parking lot two blocks from the bank.

The streetlights flickered half-dead, throwing shadows across the buildings.

No words passed between us.

Just sharp eyes, quiet nerves, and a whole lot of waiting.

I sank lower in my seat, watching Boone's jaw clench as he scanned the bank.

Every second stretched out, the quiet was heavy.

We were on edge, like two wolves circling something dangerous and alive.

A pair of headlights swept across the lot, catching the side of Boone's jaw like a flashbulb. My stomach dropped.

The car slowed—too slow—as it crept past the Nissan. For a second, I thought about ducking, but I stayed still, my pulse hammering in my ears. Finally, it turned onto

the main road and disappeared.

Boone smirked like it was nothing.

I kept watching the dark, waiting for the next set of

lights.

But we stayed parked in that cracked lot from dawn till

lunchtime, gathering every scrap of info we could.

Deliveries, employees, customers—nothing got missed.

And we were never caught.

When the lunch rush died down, we moved

closer—about a block away, still hidden in the shadows.

From then till eight o'clock, we mapped cameras,

registers, and vault locations.

This was the biggest job we'd ever tackled by far. It wore

us down, draining every ounce of focus and patience out

of us.

Eventually, Boone had to talk me down, swear we'd seen enough.

I gave in, even though my gut wasn't ready, and we packed up, headed back to the motel for one last night together.

Sometimes I wonder if we should've stayed a little longer, watched just a bit more.

Maybe it would've changed things.

Perhaps it could've saved us.

The motel room felt smaller than before; maybe the walls were just closing in on us.

Boone didn't waste any time as he opened the motel door. He began to rip his clothes off, and I followed suit. The door slammed shut behind us as our clothes fell to the floor.

This was our routine, our ritual.

But tonight felt different, more intoxicating.

He pushed me against the wall, a little too hard, but I didn't mind.

His fingers wrapped around my throat—not rough, not cruel.

Just enough to make me look him in the eye.

He was controlled. Careful. It was like he just wanted to feel my pulse under his thumb, like he needed to know I was real. That was it.

Every inch of my body was pulsing. This is what he did to me.

He drove me absolutely crazy; he had his spell over me, and there wasn't a damn thing I could do about it.

He kissed me like he'd been holding his breath all day.

Like he was starvin' for something only I could give.

His mouth moved down my neck, across my chest, hitting all the right places.

My hands in his deep auburn hair, pulling, needing more... needing him to stay in this moment and nowhere else.

We stumbled to the bed, half-naked, breathless.

He pinned me there, his body heavy over mine, but it wasn't about control.

It was the only thing holdin' us steady, keepin' us from floatin' straight into the storm waitin' on the other side of sunrise.

His hands gripped my hips like he was scared to let go. My nails dug into his back like they would hold the moment still. Like it would keep him from becoming the monster he always is when we do our jobs.

We laid there after, chest to chest, soaked in sweat and silence.

He kissed my temple. "I love you, Sugar."

"I love you."

The motel room was already cooling, but I still felt the heat between us—wild, desperate, alive.

Boone's breath evened out beside me. Mine never did.

Not that night.

My eyes fluttered shut, and I held onto that feeling, that moment, because somewhere, deep down, I knew it wouldn't last.

Chapter Ten: Cornbread Kisses

Past

The sky had been building something all afternoon that day—thick gray clouds stacking like walls, the air heavy with that wet, metallic scent that comes before a hard rain. Somewhere far off, thunder rolled low, like the earth was warning us to hurry.

This was my favorite memory of Boone and me, which happened back in East Arizona.

We slipped into that busted-up grocery store like a couple of thieves, grabbin' some real good food for a special dinner he wouldn't say nothin' about.

I didn't know what the occasion was, but I liked the mystery… It kind of made the whole night feel like more than just another damn blur of runnin' and hidin'.

The old car we had at that time wasn't working, so we had to run like hell back to our motel. We should've been pissed, cussin' up a storm… but we were belly laughing so hard we almost couldn't run.

When we finally made it to the motel on foot, we warmed up the beans slowly in the rusty skillet; the sweet smell filled the cramped room. The cornbread was still warm, crumbly, and butter-soft—nothing fancy, but it was ours.

"It smells delicious, Sugar."

I let out a little smile.

Being with Boone Bishop was a wild ride, but damn if he wasn't a true sweetheart underneath all that rough.

"It's ready, come get some, babe!"

We ate with our hands, sitting cross-legged on the bed, the stale motel air mixed with the warm scent of baked beans and cornbread.

For a minute, it felt like something close to normal—like maybe we weren't just two runaways tryin' to hold onto whatever scraps of peace we could find.

When we finished, wiping our hands on the worn rags, Boone dropped to one knee right there on that cracked motel carpet, pulling out a small silver ring with a ruby stone—my favorite color.

It was perfect. Rough around the edges, just like Boone.

"Audie Rose Carter," he said, his voice low, steady, like he was saying a prayer, "I know our love's complicated. I know this ain't no real ring, and we ain't gonna have no fancy weddin'. But I wanna call you my wife. I wanna make you mine, no matter what hell we're runnin' from. So, what do you say, darlin'?"

My chest swelled, and I felt tears prick the corners of my eyes.

"Oh my God, Boone," I whispered, breathless.

Before I could say more, I snatched the ring from his hand, slipping it on my finger like it belonged there all along.

"It *is* a real ring, Boone," I said, half-laughing, half-crying.

"And a normal weddin'… I don't want none of that fancy shit. All I want is you. Everything I got with you is perfect, Boone Bishop."

He smiled—real, soft, the kind of smile that didn't come easily for him.

He pulled me close, and for a moment, the world stopped spinning.

Just us, and that small ring shining in the dim motel light.

I didn't give a damn how Boone got that ring. It didn't matter.

What mattered was that he got it, gave it to me, and from that moment on, it was mine.

That was the best damn moment of my life.

And I wish I could've held onto it forever.

* * *

Outside, the wind died, and the whole world went still.

The kind of still that doesn't last.

Boone made the softest kind of love to me that night, like I was something sacred.

Almost like he'd been rough with the world too long and just wanted to be gentle with me.

That was the moment I knew that there was no running

from Boone.

He was mine, and I was his, and in our fucked up way…

it was one beautiful love story.

Chapter Eleven: Bullet for Boone

Present

We woke before dawn, but the world already felt off. Thick, heavy, like the air itself was waiting for something to break.

The sky was a bruised purple, and the shadows were clawing at the edges of the sunrise.

Boone broke the quiet without looking at me.

"Feels like the kind of day people don't come back from," he said, low, almost like he was talking to himself.

The words stuck in my chest like a splinter.

I could still see it in my mind... the house in Charleston right on the beach, glowing faintly through a fog of my poor-girl dreams.

Were we going there?

Or was it just some cruel fantasy that was going to slip

through our fingers, just like everything else in our lives?

The silence between us was tight, loaded with the weight

of what was coming.

The nerves subsided for the most part. We had staked out

the bank all day the previous day, hour by hour, shift by

shift.

We'd mapped that bank like it was a war zone.

We knew the holes. The faces. We weren't guessing.

When we pulled into the alley, Boone handed me a black

mask. His fingers brushed mine, slow and soft, like

maybe they wanted to stay there. In that quiet gesture, I

felt more than a plan—I felt devotion, fear, and

something even deeper.

It was like he was handing me a part of himself. Showing me the one piece of him, he could never truly explain with words.

I hesitated for a heartbeat before pulling the mask over my tangled, dirty blonde hair. The fabric was warm and soft against my dry skin.

We walked hand-in-hand from the alley to the side entrance, like we were heading into a diner instead of a full-blown heist.

The bank's heavy steel door slid open, pulling me into a harsh flood of fluorescent light and a silence so thick I could almost taste the tension.

Every step echoed loudly in my chest, but all I could focus on was Boone—solid and steady beside me, fierce and quiet like he owned this chaos.

And in that moment, his presence lit a fire inside me. A wild, stubborn kind of confidence only desperation and damage-rooted loyalty can give.

I wasn't scared anymore. Hell no.

I was ready to own every second of this chaos, take what was ours, and never look back.

Before anyone had time to scream, we moved.

Boone raised his shotgun, which he bought just for this, and took out the first guard behind the desk with a single blast to the chest.

I didn't hesitate—my pistol was already raised.

The second guard reached for his belt, and I shot him twice.

One to the gut. One to the throat.

He gurgled and collapsed against the wall, smearing red down the pale marble as he slid.

"EVERYONE ON THE FUCKING FLOOR!" Boone shouted, voice cutting through the chaos like a blade.

I bolted for the counter, jumped over it, and headed for the vault.

Then it happened—so fast I barely had time to register it.

A man in a slick suit, one of the managers, ran straight toward the silent alarm hidden behind the desk.

He made it halfway…

Boone didn't wait.

He stepped forward, raised his shotgun, and fired point-blank.

The man's chest exploded a foot in front of me.

His blood sprayed across my mask, my arms, and the vault in front of me. It dripped down the front of my jacket, warm and thick, soaking into the collar.

I didn't flinch. Well, not like I would've before.

Not like the girl who once cried over Jack's blood on her hands.

I turned back to the vault and punched in the code.

Red.

Denied.

I did it again.

Same thing.

"Fuck," I said under my breath and turned back to the audience we had.

Sirens wailed faintly in the distance—they were too close already.

I fired once into the glass ceiling, the sound deafening in the enclosed space.

The glass cracked, then shattered, raining down in sharp, glittering shards. It was quite beautiful, honestly. And Boone stood tall in the center of it all like he'd been born for this kind of sharp storm.

"WHO KNOWS THE FUCKING CODE?!" I screamed, eyes scanning the floor.

Boone looked at me through the chaos, and in that split second, something in his eyes softened.

And for just that breath of a moment, he looked the most in love I'd ever seen him.

Like I was the most special woman that existed in the world.

We snapped back into reality.

Boone turned to a man crawling toward the door and kicked him flat to the floor.

"Talk," he growled. "Now, or you're next."

A woman sobbed and held up her shaking hand.

"Three-seven-five-nine," she whispered. "Please... please just take what you want and go."

I punched in the code.

Click.

The vault door swung open like it had been waiting for me.

I tore through *everything*, stacking bundles of hundreds into our duffel bags like my life depended on it—because it did.

Four bags, packed tight with more money than we'd ever seen.

Enough to disappear.

Enough to be ghosts in Charleston.

Enough to *finally* breathe.

Boone was backing toward me now, shotgun still raised, his body tense, eyes sharp.

"Go!" I shouted.

He nodded once.

Then we ran. We didn't look back. Just bolted.

Out the back, into the alley, the car waited with the engine humming low, and the trunk cracked just enough.

We were feet from *freedom*.

Then the gunfire started.

Not from a distance.

Close.

Too fucking close.

With no damn warning.

I dropped instantly, hitting the asphalt hard, and rolled under the car. Sparks flew as bullets tore through metal, cracking concrete, infecting the air with debris.

My ears rang. My throat closed.

"Boone!" I cried. "Get down!"

But he didn't.

He couldn't.

Then I heard it—the stiff, horrible sound of a body hitting pavement.

Hard.

Final.

I screamed, then crawled out, not caring if I was next.

And there he was.

All sprawled on the ground, face pale, lips pressed tight like he was holding back a scream.

His shotgun had skidded several feet away.

Blood was pouring out from beneath him, fast and heavy, pooling around him like it belonged to the pavement.

"Boone! BOONE!"

I dropped to my knees, grabbed his face with shaking hands.

"Where is it?" I begged. "Where are you hit?"

His skin was ice. His jaw clenched.

"Hip... I think. Can't feel my leg. Can't fucking move it."

He choked on a breath, eyes wild with pain.

"Go. Take the bags. Drive. Leave—"

"Don't you *dare* say that to me."

I ripped off my jacket and pressed it to the wound, but blood soaked through in seconds.

"I'm not leaving you. Shut the hell up and hold on."

He didn't fight me. Not this time.

I hooked my arms under his and dragged him to the car with everything I had left.

He groaned, cursed, nearly blacked out along the way—then let out a scream so raw, so full of pain, it carved itself into my chest.

The kind of scream you never forget.

I finally got him into the passenger seat, slammed the door, and ran around to the driver's side.

I pressed the pedal down, the engine roared to life, and the tires bit into the cracked asphalt as we shot out of the alley.

Every nerve in my body was on fire. Adrenaline and dread mixed into a bitter cocktail that left my throat burning and my hands shaking at the wheel.

Boone's shallow breaths rattled beside me, blood still oozing from his waist.

"We're not done," I whispered, more to myself than him.

"Not yet. Not like this. Stay with me. You have to stay with me."

Behind us, the sirens were growing louder. Lights were flashing around the corner.

But I didn't look back.

I floored it.

The city blurred past.

Streetlights, parked cars, the endless maze of nowhere.
But I only saw one thing: the *last* chance we had to make
it out alive.

I wasn't about to let that slip through my fingers. But the
road ahead shimmered in the heat, warping and bending
like it was already trying to swallow us whole.

Chapter Twelve: Salt in Our Wounds

Past

"Boone, you see this?"

"What's that?"

"A beach house in South Carolina. It's beautiful, ain't it?"

"Yeah, but how the hell are we gonna get there with our twenty bucks? Are you up to doing more jobs, or are you still crying about the last one?"

"I'll do whatever it takes to get there. That's peace. That's freedom."

It was this tiny white shack right on the snow-white sand, tucked into the edge of the page like a secret waiting to be found.

The bank had a hold of it, of course, but maybe—just maybe—we could work something out.

That's what I told myself anyway.

It looked like the kind of place where people got baptized. Where everything that hurt you stayed behind in the salt.

It was so damn cute and tropical, it almost felt like it was calling out to us: *This is where you come to be saved.*

And maybe we could've been.

But we never got the chance to find out.

Arizona didn't have what South Carolina did.

Arizona was all cracked ground, dead air, and coyote howls in the dark. Dust, dirt, and a sky that didn't care if you made it out alive.

But Charleston… Charleston was green. It was a place with soft edges. The ocean on one side, the mountains on the other. It had seasons. Not like up north, but enough to feel like time moved forward instead of slipping through the cracks.

The moment I saw that beach shack, right there on that faded flyer at the gas station, I got stuck on it.

I was *hooked.*

I started checking listings like it was a religion.

Daydreaming through bloodshot eyes.

It wasn't a poor girl's dream… It was an obsession.

Probably because it was the opposite of the life I was living.

The opposite of stolen wallets, bruised arms, and motel carpets that smelled like piss and smoke. That motel smoke wasn't just on the walls—it got in your hair, your clothes, your skin. The kind that followed you out the door, like trouble you couldn't scrub off.

But one night, Boone came back late to our RV, the one we'd stolen, and he sat down at the table like he was carrying the weight of the world.

He only got serious like that when something was really heavy on his mind, so I settled in across from him, waiting.

He pulled out a worn leather wallet, cracked and faded, edges frayed like it had seen every kind of trouble.

He flipped it open slowly, then set it down in front of me—inside, a faded photo of a white sandy beach, the ocean stretched wide beneath a low sun.

"Charleston," he said, voice quiet but steady. "This is what we're chasing?"

He studied me like he was taking inventory—how tired I was, how much I still wanted it anyway. Boone had a way of sizing up the stakes without saying a word, the kind of read that came from too many nights looking over his shoulder.

I stared at the photo, the colors muted but alive in that worn snapshot.

The way the sun hung low, casting long shadows across the sand—it felt like a promise.

Like maybe, for once, there was something out there worth holding onto.

Boone's eyes met mine, hard and honest.

I nodded my head.

"No matter what, Audie," he said, voice rough but certain, "we're gonna get there. Or die trying."

I reached out, tracing the edge of the wallet with my thumb, feeling the weight of that quiet hope settle between us.

For a moment, the desert, the dust, all the broken things that had been chasing us faded away.

It was just us and that damn dream of a shore where maybe we could finally breathe.

And somewhere out there, past the dust and the heat, I swore I could smell salt in the air—like the ocean was closer than we thought, even if it was just another figment of my imagination.

Chapter Thirteen: Charleston Shore

Present

We finally made it to Charleston, but Boone's eyes were barely flickering open.

Every shallow breath he took was a fight.

All I could do was focus on finding that damn house, our last hope. A place where I could patch him up, even if it was only for a little while.

We couldn't stay long. I knew that deep down.

By now, our faces were plastered everywhere—wanted posters, news reports, maybe even the radio blaring our names like curses.

They were still out there, hunting us. Waiting.

But here, on this stretch of salty air, I clung to the fragile hope that maybe—we could catch a breath before everything came crashing down.

I eased the car onto the narrow street where the house waited, tucked behind old oaks draped in Spanish moss. It was the kind of place that looked like it had been standing still for a hundred years, untouched.

The porch sagged a little, paint peeling like sunburned skin—nothing like the photo, where it stood bright and clean against a cloudless sky. Back then, the shutters were crisp white, the railing straight, the wood gleaming like it had just been sealed.

Now the screen door hung crooked, wheezing in the breeze, and sand had etched itself into every windowpane. The boards to the porch were warped and weary, like the whole house had aged a decade in just a few seasons.

I parked with tremblin' hands, heart pounding louder than the engine's idle.

Boone fell into me, his weight solid, like a stone settling after a long fall.

I reached out and snatched the keys from the ignition.

Inside, the air smelled faintly of salt and old wood—clean, but tired from years of standing still.

I helped Boone to the worn couch and laid him down, pressing a damp cloth to his forehead.

He looked at me, eyes heavy, but managed a weak smile paired with an even weaker wink.

"We made it," he whispered.

I nodded, swallowing the lump in my throat.

"For now."

He puckered his lips, wanting a kiss, and I gave him one.

Long, soft, sincere.

Outside, the ocean whispered its warnings, but inside that fragile house, we had a moment—a breath.

I lifted his shirt to see the wound, and it was worse than I'd imagined—deep and ragged, slicing into the upper curve of his hip like a jagged bite.

A dark stain seeped through the fabric, spreading slowly, thick and warm beneath the thin fabric.

The blood was sticky, heavy with heat, clinging to my skin as I pressed against his flesh.

"Hold still," I whispered, voice rough and shaky.

My hands shook as I tore strips from the bottom of my shirt, the fabric rough and fraying. I ran them under the cold sink water, squeezing out as much as I could before folding them carefully over the wound.

I pressed the makeshift bandage tight against the gash, fighting to slow the bleeding.

Boone's eyes fluttered shut, his jaw clenched tight like he was trying to swallow the pain, but his body betrayed him, and a tremble rippled through his frame.

"I'm right here," I breathed, fingers trembling as I wrapped the cloth, twisting and knotting it as tightly as I could without cutting off circulation.

I gritted my teeth and pressed harder, my palms slick with blood. I kept wrapping until the flow slowed to a trickle instead of a flood.

It was enough... for now.

Boone's shallow breaths steadied, and though his skin was cold beneath my hands, the bleeding had stopped.

"Weed. Alcohol. Something. NOW!" he gasped, voice rough and desperate.

"Just hold on," I hissed, clenching my fists to stop them from shaking.

Then I grabbed a blunt from our stash, lighting it slowly, letting the smoke curl between us—an ugly kind of comfort in the chaos.

I rummaged through the cabinets filled with dusty cans, hoping to find some wine, but found a can of chili instead. The expiration date had faded, but I knew it had to be bad, like all the other food in there.

"Fuck it," I muttered under my breath as I poured it into an old bowl to heat up.

The microwave made this low, haunted growl as it came to life. Everything in that house felt haunted, tired, forgotten, on the edge of giving out.

Just like us.

I leaned against the counter while the bowl spun. My hands were still shaking, and smoke lingered in the air from the blunt. The potent smell mixed with the faint, metallic smell of blood.

Boone's blood.

When it beeped, I jumped. Stupid. I was jumpy as hell.

I grabbed the bowl with the corner of what was left of my shirt and carried it into the living room.

Boone was still slumped on the couch, head tilted to the side, chest rising just enough to prove he was alive, barely.

The pieces of my cream shirt pressed to his side had gone to a dark maroon... the kind of color you don't come back from.

"Here," I said softly, kneeling beside him. "I found some food."

He blinked slowly, like even that took effort. His skin was as pale as a ghost. His lips were dry and cracked, turning a shade of purple.

He looked like something unraveling, something decaying.

"I'm not hungry," he whispered.

"I know," I said. "It's not about that. It's about staying alive. And here. With me."

I stirred the chili, blew on a spoonful, and held it up. He looked at it, then at me. Like he wanted to take it just to make me feel better.

His lips barely parted. I fed him a bite. He chewed slowly, then swallowed like it hurt.

"Good," I whispered. "That's good, baby."

Another bite. Then he coughed it all up, with some blood. He curled forward just a little before falling back again, gasping.

"I got you," I said, sliding in close so his head could rest against my chest. I held the bowl with one hand, the other cradling him like something breakable.

Something already broke.

He didn't speak for a while. Then he said, real quiet, "You remember Georgia? That field with all those peaches. How you dared me to fill my pockets with em."

I let out a sigh with a faint giggle that felt like it had been stuck in my lungs for years.

"I remember. You ended up with about twenty and smelled like sugar for three days."

He gave the faintest smile, but it didn't reach his eyes.

"I thought about that today," he said. "Right before I fell. I thought, if I die, I wanna remember somethin' sweet and pure."

My throat closed up. I couldn't say anything.

"I'm sorry, Audie," he murmured, barely there.

"For all the ways I hurt you."

I shook my head. "Don't. Not now, Boone."

He didn't argue. He just closed his eyes, and for a second, I thought he was gone.

But then he whispered, "I wish I could've given you somethin' better."

I held him tighter, pressed a kiss to his forehead, and let the tears fall freely.

"You gave me you, and that was all I ever wanted." Tears snuck out before I had a chance to stop them.

The bowl sat forgotten, untouched.

The house creaked around us, the way old places do when they're trying to hold in all the ghosts and forbidden secrets.

Then I noticed it.

A record player, hidden in the corner, half-covered in dust and shadow. The kind with wood paneling and a cracked leather speaker. It looked ancient. Forgotten.

Boone followed my gaze, his voice a rasp.

"Bet it still works."

"Boone—"

"Help me up."

"No."

"C'mon, baby," he said, forcing a crooked smile. "One last dance."

I wanted to tell him no again, that he was gonna tear himself open worse. That this wasn't the time. That we didn't need a damn dance. But I couldn't.

Not with the way he looked at me, like he needed it. Like this was the thing he wanted to do with whatever time he had left.

And deep down, I think I knew that would be our last dance, and so I slid my arm under his and braced him as he pushed himself off the couch with a groan that made my whole body tense.

He swayed into me, heavy and trembling, like his body was already halfway gone. But his eyes were still locked on mine, stubborn and soft, full of something that looked a lot like goodbye.

He looked at me the way you look at a photograph you know you'll never see again—like he was already memorizing me.

I crossed the room and flipped open the lid of the record player. There was already a vinyl inside—dull black, unlabeled, warped at the edges. I didn't care. I set the needle down and prayed it would play.

The speakers crackled to life.

Then came the soft hum of a steel guitar—slow, haunting—and Hank Williams Jr.'s voice drifted in with "Outlaw's Reward," like he was right there in the room, offering one last song for the dying.

Boone's mouth curled into a weak, crooked smile.

It twisted my stomach, that smile of his, even as he was dying.

"Guess that's fitting," he rasped.

He held out his arms, and I went to him, like always.

We moved slowly, barely more than a sway, my arms tight around his ribs, his breath hot and uneven against my neck.

His strength was failing, but he kept dancing. Kept going.

For me.

But soon the sirens started.

Soft at first. Then louder, screeching violently.

But in that moment, it was just us and that sad old song for being the kind of man no one ever gave a second chance to.

Boone whispered, "You remember this one? I used to make you listen to it on repeat—back when we thought being outlaws meant somethin' romantic."

I nodded, choking on the lump in my throat.

"It was romantic," I said. "You made it that way."

The lights flashed through the window—red, blue, red, blue—painting our skin in the colors.

Then his knees buckled.

He dropped in my arms, and I fell with him, dragging us both to the floor.

"BOONE!" I didn't think. I pressed my hands to his side, screaming his name again, my knees slipping in his blood as the sirens roared closer.

The scene looked comparable to all the bloodbaths we'd created—same smell, same heat leaving the body too fast.

We'd run out of time—no more dances, no goodbye.

Chapter Fourteen: Empty Cradle

Past

The sun blistered the earth to ash, turning the desert into a kiln that never cooled. The air outside shimmered with heat, and inside the RV, it was worse—thick, stale, tinged with the faint bite of old cigarette smoke that never really left your lungs. Sweat slid down my spine, sticky and constant, making the walls feel closer by the hour.

Boone hadn't said much since that night, the night he killed the old man who owned that rig. I didn't say much either.

We both knew better. That was just how we had to get by.

Inside, the air was stale, and the windows were streaked with dirt.

Every morning in that tight bathroom, closing my eyes, I'd fight the nausea that was trying to twist my gut.

I wasn't sure if it was the smell of this place, the lack of food, or the heat, but I was constantly nauseous.

It was there. All the time.

After a month of fighting the nausea, Boone went out for a solo job, so I walked to the nearest gas station and finally bought a pregnancy test. I took it right there in their bathroom so Boone wouldn't see the trash, but that didn't end up mattering.

After two minutes of waiting, there were two solid lines.

I was so shocked.

"Shit," I said out loud.

We were two kids ourselves, criminals at that.

A baby. I knew it was reckless—dangerous in a way.

But when I saw those two lines, my chest tightened and my mind went numb. I couldn't stop the wave of joy crashing through me, even if a part of me screamed that it was all wrong.

On the walk back to the RV, I replayed every way I could tell Boone. My heart hammered.

Would he hate me? Love me? Be scared like I was?

I didn't know.

Hell, I barely knew how I felt.

When I stepped inside, I held up the test slowly, revealing the secret only I kept.

Boone's eyes filled with tears—real tears. Not the tough ones he wore like armor, but soft, honest ones.

For once, hope didn't feel like a cruel joke.

It didn't seem so far out of reach.

"Oh God, Audie... I'm gonna be a dad. We're gonna be parents." His voice cracked, breaking through the silence with something tender, something new.

I nodded, swallowing hard, tears pooling behind my eyes.

"I still can't believe it!"

We talked all night about girl names. We quickly decided on Rosie Arizona Bishop. Honoring me and our home state, since we were planning on heading to Charleston.

It all felt right, like the pieces were falling into place.

* * *

We only went to the doctor twice, but the doctor even talked about how healthy she was.

At the second appointment, we found out officially that it was a girl.

The stars just kept aligning.

For three months, I let myself believe.

I watched Boone relax into it, too, even if it was just a little.

We clung to a dream we never once spoke—like saying it might break it.

Then one night, Boone was gone, hunting or hustling or whatever dangerous thing he had to do.

I sat alone as the cramps came, sharp and cruel.

I stumbled to the bathroom, my breath caught in my throat. When I saw the blood, a cold ache hollowed in my chest.

My baby was dying inside me, and I couldn't do anything about it.

No car, no phone, no Boone. Ten miles from the nearest hospital.

I was too far and out of luck.

I curled up on the bed, clutching my belly like it was the last piece of hope I had left. I whispered to her, to Rosie—soft promises, prayers, apologies.

And I cried until there was nothing left but silence.

I like to say I held my baby as she passed—because I did.

Boone stepped inside, brushing dust from his shirt, smirking just a little. "You wouldn't believe the deal I just worked, Audie. Coulda gone bad, but I made 'em see my way."

When he finally focused his eyes on me, I saw his shoulders sink low, and his face became a blank canvas.

He didn't ask or say a word. He quickly connected the dots.

Then the rage came—raw, harsh—not at me, but at the world that stole our chance.

He tore through the RV like a storm, throwing plates, punching walls, trying to break something—anything to make it all better.

And then, just like that, he stopped, dropped to the floor, and cried.

I dropped beside him, wrapping my arms around his shaking body, feeling his pain like my own.

"I wanted her so bad, Audie. I wanted to be Rosie's dad so bad."

I wanted to cry all over again, but I held it back.

"I know, Boone. Life's fucking cruel. And it doesn't make sense. I don't know. Maybe this is the world punishing us... two broken souls who didn't deserve her."

"That's bullshit," he yelled, voice breaking.

"There are plenty of people out there who shouldn't have kids. But us? We would've been the best, because we know what not to be. You know that."

I couldn't stop the sobs then, my whole body aching with loss and regret.

"Well, Boone... maybe we just aren't meant to have kids."

It wasn't meant to hurt him, but it was the only way I could get through to him.

"Just throw the cradle away, I can't look at it."

I watched his face crumble like it was made of glass.

And mine broke right along with it, but I swallowed the shards down.

Maybe it was better this way.

Maybe we weren't meant to bring a baby into this broken, godforsaken world.

That was what I had to keep telling myself anyway, and that's what I've told myself every day since.

Boone and I never spoke of her again after that; Rosie was just another broken piece of us.

Chapter Fifteen: Echoes of Us

Present

Boone's head laid heavy in my lap, and I ran my fingers softly through his hair. I traced his face with trembling hands, singing along quietly to the song still playing in the background.

He was dying.

His breath slowed, his pulse grew faint, and his skin looked like it belonged to someone already buried.

Tears welled in my eyes, spilling over as memories crashed through me. I wondered if those were the same memories replaying in his mind right then.

As soon as his heart stopped beating, and he let out his final breath, there was a knock at the door.

"POLICE! OPEN UP!"

Our time was up.

No more running.

No more hiding.

Our little dance had gone on too long, and the past had finally caught us.

It was the end of us.

I reached for Boone's hip—his right one, where he always kept his shiny revolver.

There was one bullet left, *lucky me.*

My hand trembled, fingers curling around the grip like it was the only thing keeping me tethered to this world.

I looked at Boone and pressed one last kiss to his lips, already stiff and cold as ice.

Already not Boone.

The door splintered open, police flooding through the narrow hallway, their boots thudding against the creaky floorboards. I could hear them shouting, voices close, urgent—closing in.

I raised the gun to my temple... and *pulled the trigger*.

The light slipped out of my sight, and my body hit the floor with a heavy thud that echoed through the entire house.

Memories flooded my mind—Boone and me, Aria and Ayla, and a few of my momma and daddy.

My vision blurred, fading fast, but I saw Boone's body one last time—still, silent, a shadow in the flickering light.

And in that moment, peace—true peace—washed over me.

Epilogue

It was a mean, gray day—the kind that crawls under your skin and sits there.

Been like that all week. The rain doesn't stop. Fog thick as grief.

I've been working at this old roadside diner for nearly two years now.

Found it right after I found out the truth about Audie.

About how she died.

About how she lived.

She and Boone ate here once, back when they were still running, still in love, still dreaming wild.

I came here to ask the manager some questions, get some answers my momma refused to give me.

Ended up never leavin'.

It was like something in the walls wanted me to stay.

Maybe it was Audie, maybe it was the voices in my head.

Folks come in sometimes, order pie and coffee, and ask about 'em.

The outlaw lovers.

The Ballad of Audie & Boone.

They say it like it's some story spun outta thin air—romantic, tragic, a little dangerous.

But they don't know the half of it.

I do.

Because I'm her sister.

I was just a girl when she left.

Now I'm twenty, older than Audie was when she died.

That's the part that don't sit right. She was only eighteen, Boone twenty-one.

But I know deep in my bones that she'd be proud of me.

She was always proud of Aria and me, even when she couldn't show it.

Even when the world kept her too far away.

I still remember her voice, low and sweet, singing under her breath when she thought no one was listening.

I still feel her in the wind that blows through my hair when the car windows are down, and when the song plays too perfectly on the jukebox.

She's here, in the stories folks tell and the silence between 'em.

She's on the walls of this diner. And in me.

Audie Rose Carter should've been Bishop. A legend. A badass.

My sister. And proud to say it.

She was a damn fire that burned too fast, too bright.

She loved Boone like it was the only thing she knew how to do.

And he loved her right back—bloody, broken, and all in.

They were a storm together. And storms never last.

But damn if they didn't leave a mark.

So yeah, I'm pouring coffee now. Wiping down tables.

Listenin' to folks speak her name like it came from a ghost story.

Like her story is some mournful, twisted ballad meant to outlive her.

And I let 'em, most of the time.

'Cause maybe that's what she wanted.

To be remembered.

And Lord, she is.

Every time the rain falls, every time that steel guitar cries from the speakers, every time someone leans in and asks: "Y'all ever hear what really happened to Audie and Boone?"

I usually just smile and top off their cup.

But now and then—when the folks don't get the story right—I'll play along.

Some folks I'll correct, and some I'll bury. It just depends on how they tell it.

For you, Audie.

Always for you.